KLAUS BAUMGART lives with his family in Berlin. The LAURA'S STAR series has had multi-million sales worldwide, and has been broadcast on TV throughout Europe, including in the UK, and the first title, LAURA'S STAR, has been made into a film. Klaus Baumgart was the first German author/illustrator to be shortlisted for the Children's Book Award in 1999 for LAURA'S STAR.

Also available by Klaus Baumgart:

Picture Books
LAURA'S STAR
LAURA'S CHRISTMAS STAR
LAURA'S SECRET
First Reader
LAURA'S STAR AND THE NEW TEACHER
Activity Book
LAURA'S STAR STICKER ACTIVITY BOOK

LITTLE TIGER PRESS
An imprint of Magi Publications
1 The Coda Centre, 189 Munster Road, London SW6 6AW
www.littletigerpress.com

First published in Great Britain 2005

A CIP catalogue record for this book is available from the British Library

ISBN 1 84506 207 8

Printed in China

4 6 8 10 9 7 5 3

Laura's Star

and the Sleepover

Klaus Baumgart

English text by Fiona Waters

LITTLE TIGER PRESS
London

Important Plans

"Let's talk about all the things we're going to do this weekend," Laura said. She was sitting in her room with her best friend, Sophie. Laura had a sheet of paper in front of her and at the top of the page she'd written 'Things to Do'.

Tomorrow, Laura and Sophie were going to stay with Sophie's

Aunt Jenny, who had a house by the sea. Laura was very excited because she had never stayed away from home without her mum and dad and little brother Tommy before.

"Well," Sophie began, "we can stay up really late, if we want. We can have a midnight feast and eat chocolate biscuits. Before that, we'll go to the beach and build sand sculptures. If it's nice and sunny, we can go swimming and paddling in the rock pools."

"Stop, stop!" Laura cried. "I can't write that quickly, you know."

So Sophie began again more slowly, while Laura wrote everything down. Just then Tommy came in.

"What are you two doing?"
he asked.

"We're planning our sleepover,"
said Laura. "We don't want to
forget anything!"

Tommy listened carefully as
Sophie went through the list.

"I want to have a midnight feast and go to the beach too," said Tommy.

"You can't, Tommy," said Sophie. "You aren't coming."

"But I want to!" Tommy replied.

Laura groaned. Sometimes her little brother could be really annoying, especially now, when she had so many important things to discuss with Sophie.

"You're far too little to stay up till midnight. In fact, I don't even think you could stay awake that long," said Laura.

"I could, too!" Tommy shouted crossly. "It isn't fair. You get to do everything!"

He stormed out of the room,
slamming the door behind him.

Later, when Sophie had gone,
Laura went to see Tommy.
He was in his room playing with
his bulldozer. When
Laura came in he
turned his back
on her.

"Tommy," she said softly, "don't be upset. I didn't mean it like that."

Tommy sniffed and said, "I'm not upset. It just isn't fair. I want a midnight feast, too."

Laura thought for a moment. "I know!" she said. "You and I can have a midnight feast, this evening."

Tommy turned round. "This evening? Do you mean it?"

Laura nodded.

"With chocolate biscuits?"

Laura nodded again.

"All right then," said Tommy happily. "When can we start?"

"At midnight, Tommy," Laura answered. "Midnight feasts always start at midnight."

A Midnight Feast
for Tommy

"Are you sure that you've got
everything ready for tomorrow?"
Mum asked Laura that evening.

"Oh yes," said Laura, "I've got
my paints, pencils and my torch."

"Have you got your swimming
costume?" Mum asked.

"Yes, I have," Laura said.

"And your pyjamas?"

"Of course I have," said Laura.

"How about your anorak in case it rains?"

"Hmm, I'm not quite sure . . ."

"I'll check everything with you," Mum offered.

* * *

At supper Tommy announced, "Laura and I are having a midnight feast later."

Dad raised his eyebrows. "Don't forget that Laura has to get up early tomorrow morning, Tommy, and you look quite tired yourself."

"But Laura promised me, didn't you, Laura?"

Laura nodded, but she wasn't sure it was such a good idea any more. It was only seven o'clock now – five hours until midnight.

"Maybe you could have your midnight feast a little earlier, Tommy," Mum suggested.

"No," said Tommy. "It must be midnight to have a midnight feast. That's what Laura said."

Suddenly Laura had a wonderful idea!

* * *

Tommy was sitting on his bed in his pyjamas when Laura came into his room later that evening. She was carrying a tray with biscuits and two mugs of hot chocolate on it – and her alarm clock. She'd turned the knob on the back of her clock until both hands pointed to twelve.

"Look, Tommy, it's midnight!" said Laura. "It's time for our feast!"

"Wow, midnight already. I've never been up this late, Laura," said Tommy, his tired smile turning into a big grin.

Laura sat down on the bed next to Tommy and they munched and laughed together until Tommy started to yawn and yawn.

Tommy just managed to stagger into the bathroom to clean his teeth and to mumble goodnight to Laura before falling into bed.

When Laura went back to her room she saw all her things ready for the trip. Her heart pounded. She was very excited, but also a little afraid.

Laura opened her window and looked out at the night sky. Up there, among the other stars, was her friend the star, shining and gleaming down at her.

Laura waved. "Hello, Star," she called softly.

Her star waved back at her with a radiant beam of starlight.

"Guess what, Star! I'm going on a sleepover with Sophie. We're staying at her Aunt Jenny's house at the seaside."

The star twinkled and let a few glittery sparkles fly.

"Yes, I am very excited," Laura answered. "Tomorrow morning, almost before it's light, Sophie and her mum are going to pick me up in the car, and we'll drive a long, long way to the seaside. But I do feel a bit nervous, Star. I've never been away without Mummy and Daddy and Tommy before."

Laura's star shone as brightly as it could and sent cartwheels of sparkles down to Laura. Laura felt all wrapped up and cosy in her star's bright warm light. Everything would be wonderful.

At the Seaside

The next morning, Sophie and her mum came to pick Laura up. Laura hugged Mum and Dad and as she hugged Tommy she said, "I'll find a great big shell for you, the biggest one on the whole beach."

Then she got into the car and off they went. Sophie and Laura really enjoyed the journey. They chatted,

sang songs, and played I-spy and
other games with Sophie's mum,
and ate up all their sandwiches.

Just when they thought the
journey had been long enough,
Sophie's mum said, "Who's going
to be the first one to see the sea?"

Laura and Sophie craned their necks. "The sea!" they both cried, at exactly the same time. "There's the sea!"

The water glittered and sparkled. "How beautiful!" Laura thought. "It's like thousands of little stars."

Soon after, they arrived at Aunt Jenny's house. She was waiting by the door and was very pleased to see them. "Hello, did you have a good journey?" she called as they got out of the car.

Aunt Jenny was wearing a pretty orange dress and matching beads and earrings. She had lovely red hair and a huge smile. She laughed a lot and made them feel very welcome.

She took Laura and Sophie by the hand and led them into her big sunny kitchen. They all sat around the table drinking juice and talking, until Sophie's mum looked at her watch and said, "I had better be on my way. I'll pick you both up tomorrow afternoon."

They went to the car to wave goodbye, and Laura suddenly felt nervous.

"When Sophie's mum drives

away I'll have to stay here," she thought anxiously.

But the feeling was gone in a flash because Aunt Jenny suddenly cried, "Last one to the beach has to do the washing up after supper!"

Sophie and Laura grabbed their swimming things and raced down to the beach as fast as their legs could carry them, with Aunt Jenny following behind.

The beach was wonderful. The girls found the perfect place to spread out their things, and they drew pictures in the soft, golden sand.

The sea was calm with friendly little waves that tickled their feet.

They all jumped about in the sea
and played with a big beach ball.

Then, when they were tired, they
wrapped themselves in their towels
and sat on the beach watching the
waves. After they had eaten some of
Aunt Jenny's delicious sandwiches
they began their search for a huge
shell for Tommy.

Laura was delighted to find a pretty little starfish in a shallow pool. It was red and it had five points.

"It looks a bit like my star," Laura thought and glanced up into the sunny blue sky.

They had luck in their search for shells! There were so many they could hardly decide which ones to collect.

Lying in the shadow of a big rock, they found the most enormous shell they had ever seen. When you held it to your ear you could hear the sea. It  would make the perfect present for Tommy!

Laura and Sophie put the shell in their bucket, then they watched the tide filling the rock pools. They were having so much fun they didn't notice the wind growing stronger, blowing clouds across the sky.

"Come on, you two little mermaids!" called Aunt Jenny. "Let's go back to the house before it starts to rain!"

Laura and Sophie carefully
carried their shells up the beach,
planning to make necklaces with the
prettiest ones.

"They'll be brilliant!" Laura
laughed.

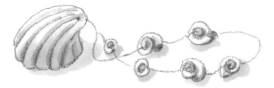

Sleepover Surprise

When they got back the girls put all of their shells in a basin to wash the salt and sand off them, then they each had a shower to wash the salt and sand off themselves!

After that they went to their room to unpack. The room was right at the top of the house in the attic and had sloping walls with big

windows that looked over the garden and sea.

Looking out of one of the windows Laura could see the darkening sky, filled with clouds racing in the wind. "I wish I could see my star," Laura thought.

They had a delicious supper and chatted with Aunt Jenny. Before they knew it, it was time for bed. They said goodnight to Aunt Jenny and clambered up the stairs with a tray of home-made cookies and juice for their midnight feast.

Laura and Sophie laid all the shells they had collected on the beds.

"This is the one I like best,"

Sophie said, showing Laura a shell
with a small hole at the top edge.

"That's just right for a
necklace," said Laura, hunting
around for another.

Laura and Sophie had a
wonderful time making jewellery.

Then they sorted shells and drew seaside pictures. Laura drew lots of little starfish.

The girls were so busy they didn't notice that the wind had strengthened. It was now howling around the chimneys and swishing the branches of the trees to and fro.

"Golly, that sounds really scary, just like a ghost!" Sophie murmured.

Laura pulled her blanket over her head and wailed, "I'm a ghost, woohoo."

Sophie giggled and pulled her blanket over her head, too. To make it even scarier they turned off the light and in the beam of Laura's torch the Sophie-ghost and the

Laura-ghost bounced up and down
on the beds.

When Laura and Sophie finally
sat down, they could hear raindrops
pattering against the window, tip,
tap, tip, tap. It sounded like
knocking, as if someone wanted to
come in. The wind seemed to have
grown even stronger. Laura quickly
turned on the main light.

"Let's have our midnight feast now," said Sophie. But just then the light flickered and went out.

"Hey, put the light back on," Laura said.

"I didn't turn it off, Laura," Sophie answered.

Grabbing Laura's torch, Sophie found the light switch, but no matter how much they switched it back and forth the light wouldn't come on.

"Oh d-dear!" Sophie stuttered. She looked at the torch. Its glow seemed fainter than when they had been playing. "What if the torch runs out? I'll go and get Aunt Jenny. If she can't fix the light, I'm sure she'll be able to find us some new batteries."

"All right," said Laura trying to sound braver than she felt.

Sophie took the torch, opened the door, and made her way down the creaky stairs. Laura sat on her bed, hugging her knees, listening to the wind and the rain. It was completely dark. Suddenly, Laura felt very afraid.

"Sophie," she whispered, "Sophie, I'll come with you!"

But Sophie had gone. Laura longed for Mum and Dad, even Tommy. But she was alone. Alone with the ghosts who were knocking on the window and hissing at her to let them in.

A Light in the Dark

Laura stared with wide-open eyes into the darkness. She couldn't do anything but wait, her heart beating wildly. She sat there and listened, growing more and more frightened. Laura felt her throat get tighter and she almost screamed.

But what was that? Gradually it seemed to be getting lighter. The

light was coming from above,
through the attic window. She
looked up and there, shining in
through the window, was her star.
Of course it was her star!

The star waved to her with a soft beam of light. The wind was blowing it from side to side but the star held on tight, its points wedged into the window frame.

Laura climbed on to the bed and opened the window. With a gust of wind and quite a few raindrops the star came tumbling into the room.

Laura breathed a deep sigh of relief. "You've arrived just in time, Star," she said.

Her star turned a few cartwheels through the air and danced. Laura laughed. She told the star all about her wonderful day by the sea, the shells they'd found and the starfish. Everything was all right now.

Then the star flew round the room and discovered just what it was looking for under the table – an old lantern! It stuck one of its points inside and shook it about. Glittering stardust powdered down and formed a little radiant cloud. The star withdrew its point and the lamp glowed with a  silvery light, gently brightening all of the shadowy corners of the room.

At that moment, Laura heard someone calling her name. "Laura, Laura, everything is all right now."

It was Sophie and Aunt Jenny.

Laura heard them coming up the creaky stairs. She gently stroked the points of her star and whispered, "What a shame. You must go now, Star, or they'll see you." She hugged the star and took it to the window.

Then she held it up, and swiftly it flew away into the darkness. Laura waved a quick farewell and closed the window.

Sophie and Aunt Jenny had brought some candles. They told Laura that a tree had fallen and brought down the power line to the house. They were sorry they had taken so long but they'd had to search for the candles and then it took ages to find the matches.

Sophie put her arm around Laura and said, "Hope you weren't as scared as I was!"

Laura replied, "I was a bit afraid at first, but I soon got over it. Look!"

She held the lantern up, so that
Sophie and Aunt Jenny could see it,
and they laughed.

"I haven't used that lantern for
ages!" said Aunt Jenny. Then she

added, "I think we need a special treat after this big scare. How about some ice-cream to go with the cookies?"

Sophie and Laura thought that was a brilliant idea. Aunt Jenny brought up three bowls and they all celebrated their midnight feast together.

Slowly the lantern began to dim and the candles burned down. Sophie was already asleep and Laura's eyes grew heavy.

Aunt Jenny blew out the candles and the little lantern. "Sleep tight, girls," she whispered. As soon as she was out of the room, the lantern lit up again with a soft, warm glow.

"Starlight," thought Laura and drifted contentedly off to sleep.

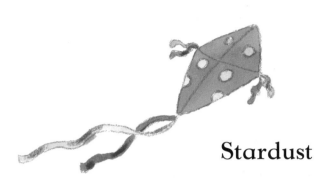

Stardust

Next morning, the electricity was
back on. After breakfast, Laura and
Sophie ran straight to the beach
because Aunt Jenny had lent them
two brightly coloured kites. They let
the kites fly way up high. Laura's
kite spiralled and circled in the sky.

"I bet my star would enjoy this,"
Laura thought, and when Sophie

wasn't looking she waved to her star up in the sky. Laura knew now that her star could see her, even when it was cloudy.

When Sophie's mum arrived to pick them up, Laura and Sophie agreed that it was much too soon to go home. They hugged Aunt Jenny and asked if they could come and visit again very soon. Aunt Jenny promised that she would have enough torches and batteries next time, just in case!

That evening, Laura spread her shells out on the kitchen table and told Mum, Dad and Tommy all about her weekend.

"We went paddling in the sea, we collected shells on the beach, and I even stroked a little starfish," she told them. "And in the night there was a storm, and the power lines were down. It was totally dark, and the light wouldn't work!" she said. "And this morning we went to the beach to fly kites. It was really windy."

Laura had done so much she felt like she'd been away for ages. She gave Tommy the big shell that she had found for him. They all took turns holding it to their ear.

"That's what the sea sounds like," Laura explained.

"Were you really, really frightened when the lights went off, Laura?" Tommy asked and looked at her with a wide-eyed gaze.

"Luckily, I wasn't alone," she said, and in her mind's eye she saw her star. She remembered the picture she had drawn of the starfish and she went and got it. As she put it on the table she noticed that all of the starfish were glittering – with stardust, sprinkled on them by her wonderful star.